The Juggle Puzzle

TREASURE BAY

Parent's Introduction

Welcome to **We Read Phonics**! This series is designed to help you assist your child in reading. Each book includes a story, as well as some simple word games to play with your child. The games focus on the phonics skills and sight words your child will use in reading the story.

Here are some recommendations for using this book with your child:

1 Word Play

There are word games both before and after the story. Make these games fun and playful. If your child becomes bored or frustrated, play a different game or take a break.

Many of the games require printed materials (for example, sight word cards). You can print free game materials from your computer by going online to www.WeReadPhonics.com and clicking on the Game Materials link for this title. However, game materials can also be easily made with paper and a marker—and making them with your child can be a great learning activity.

② Read the Story

After some word play, read the story aloud to your child—or read the story together, by reading aloud at the same time or by taking turns. As you and your child read, move your finger under the words.

Next, have your child read the entire story to you while you follow along with your finger under the words. If there is some difficulty with a word, either help your child to sound it out or wait about five seconds and then say the word.

③ Discuss and Read Again

After reading the story, talk about it with your child. Ask questions like, "What happened in the story?" and "What was the best part?" It will be helpful for your child to read this story to you several times. Another great way for your child to practice is by reading the book to a younger sibling, a pet, or even a stuffed animal!

LEVEL 6 Level 6 introduces words with "ey," "ie," and "y" with the long "e" sound (as in *key, chief,* and *sunny*), "oa," "oe," and "ow" with the long "o" sound (as in *boat, toe,* and *show*), and "ew" and "ue" with the long "u" sound (as in *crew* and *blue*). Also included are word endings -es, -ed, and -ly (as in *misses, started,* and *quickly*).

The Juggle Puzzle

A We Read Phonics™ Book
Level 6

Text Copyright © 2011 by Treasure Bay, Inc.
Illustrations Copyright © 2011 by Olga and Aleksey Ivanov

Reading Consultants: Bruce Johnson, M.Ed., and Dorothy Taguchi, Ph.D.

We Read Phonics™ is a trademark of Treasure Bay, Inc.

Published by
Treasure Bay, Inc.
P.O. Box 119
Novato, CA 94948 USA

Printed in Singapore

Library of Congress Catalog Card Number: 2011925873

PDF E-Book ISBN: 978-1-60115-591-7
Hardcover ISBN: 978-1-60115-343-2
Paperback ISBN: 978-1-60115-344-9

We Read Phonics™
Patent Pending

Visit us online at:
www.TreasureBayBooks.com

PR-6-11

The Juggle Puzzle

By Sindy McKay

Illustrated by Olga and Aleksey Ivanov

Phonics Game

Making Words

Creating words using new letter patterns will help your child read this story.

Materials:

Option 1—Fast and Easy: To print free game materials from your computer, go online to www.WeReadPhonics.com, then go to this book title and click on the link to "View & Print: Game Materials."

Option 2—Make Your Own: You'll need thick paper or cardboard, crayon or marker, and scissors. Cut 2 x 2 inch squares from the paper or cardboard and print these letters and letter patterns on the squares: oa, ew, ow, y, g, t, d, n, l, sh, ch, r, b, ck, and u.

1. Place the cards letter side up in front of your child.

2. Ask your child to make and say words using the letters available. For example, your child could choose the letters "b," "oa," and "t," and make the word *boat*.

3. If your child has difficulty, try presenting letters that will make a specific word. For example, present "g," "oa," and "t," and ask your child to make *goat*. You could then ask your child to find a letter to change the word to *boat*.

4. Ask your child to make as many words as possible that use the "oa," "ew," "ow," and "y" cards. These letter patterns are used in the story. Possible words include *goat, boat, shy, try, show, showy, boat, row, dew, chew, new, lucky,* and *road*.

Sight Word Game

Go Fish

Play this game to practice sight words used in the story.

Materials:

Option 1—Fast and Easy: To print free game materials from your computer, go online to www.WeReadPhonics.com, then go to this book title and click on the link to "View & Print: Game Materials."

Option 2—Make Your Own: You'll need 18 index cards and a marker. Write each word listed on the right on two cards. You will now have two sets of cards.

1 Using one set of cards, ask your child to repeat each word after you. Shuffle both decks of cards together, and deal three cards to each player. Put the remaining cards face down in a pile.

2 Player 1 asks player 2 for a particular word. If player 2 has the word card, then he passes it to player 1. If player 2 does not have the word card, then he says, "Go fish," and player 1 takes a card from the pile. Player 2 takes a turn.

3 Whenever a player has two cards with the same word, he puts those cards down on the table and says the word out loud. The player with the most matches wins the game.

4 Keep the cards and combine them with other sight word cards you make. Use them all to play this game or play sight word games featured in other **We Read Phonics** books.

soon

they

would

saw

could

without

know

how

juggle

Meet Side Show Dean. He is in Mister
Bob's Traveling Show. He can juggle
a tiger, a goat, and a pot of stew.

Dean must never miss or drop
them. If he did, the goat would eat
the stew.

Then the tiger would eat the goat.

Lucky for the goat, Dean never
makes a mistake or misses.

One day, Dean woke up late. Mister
Bob's Traveling Show had left without him.
Dean had to catch up with the show!

8

He saw wagon tracks. He followed
the tracks down the road.

The tracks stopped at a river. Dean saw Mister Bob's Traveling Show on the far side.

How could he reach them?

Then Dean saw a small rowboat. It could carry Dean plus one more thing. Dean had to think.

He could row the tiger across. But
then the goat would eat the stew.

He could row the stew across. But
then the tiger would eat the goat.

He could row the goat across. And
the tiger would not eat the stew.

So that is what Dean did!

Then Dean went back. Who should
he row across next?

He could row the stew across. But then the goat would eat the stew.

He could row the tiger across. But
then tiger would eat the goat!
Do you know what Dean did?

Dean went across with the stew.
He left the stew on the far side. But the
goat came back with him.

Dean left the goat alone on the first side. And the tiger went to the far side with him.

Dean left the tiger on the far side.
The tiger would not eat the stew.

Dean went back to the first side and picked up the goat. He and the goat went to the far side.

Now they are all on the same side!

Soon they will catch up with Mister Bob's Traveling Show.

Do not worry. Side Show Dean
never misses!

Phonics Game

Moving Up

Taking a careful look at the words in the story will help your child to reread those words or patterns another time or in another story.

Materials:

Option 1—Fast and Easy: To print free game materials from your computer, go online to www.WeReadPhonics.com, then go to this book title and click on the link to "View & Print: Game Materials."

Option 2—Make Your Own: You'll need 20 index cards, markers, scissors, and paper clips. Write each of the following 10 words on two index cards to make two sets of cards:

goat, stew, Dean, eat, lucky, show, road, row, boat, worry

1 Take one set of the cards and cut up the letters, but keep letter combinations together. For example, cut goat into three cards: "g," "oa," and "t." Cut the words as follows: g/oa/t, s/t/ew, D/ea/n, ea/t, l/u/ck/y, sh/ow, r/oa/d, r/ow, b/oa/t, w/or/ry.

2 Place a card that is not cut up on a table, and the matching card with the cut up letters in order about six inches below.

3 The child first reads the top word. He then slowly repeats the first sound while sliding the matching letter underneath the top letter. Continue with the remaining letters and sounds. Finish by rereading the word again.

4 To add a little bit of fun, create some nonsense words. After creating a real word, switch some of the consonants around to make some nonsense or silly words. Reread the words.

5 Paper clip the complete word to the matching cut up letters to keep for another time.

Make a Face

Help your child practice some of the words in the story.

R E A C H

Materials: paper; pencil, crayon, or marker

1. Choose one of the words from this list: *goat, eat, Dean, show, reach, boat, row, lucky, road, misses, stopped.*

2. At the bottom of the paper, draw a line for each letter in the word. For example, if the word is *reach,* draw five lines, creating a spot for each letter.

3. The child guesses a letter. If the letter is in the chosen word, put the letter on the appropriate line. For example, if the word is *reach* and the child guesses the letter "c," put the letter "c" in the fourth spot. If the letter is not in the chosen word, start to draw a face. Start with a circle for the basic face, then the eyes, then eyebrows, and so on.

4. The object of the game is for the child to guess the correct letters and the word before the face is completed. If your child has trouble, give hints, such as "Guess the letter that makes the "rrr" sound."

5. Play again with another word.

If you liked *The Juggle Puzzle,*
here is another **We Read Phonics** book you are sure to enjoy!

The Garden Crew

It's fun to grow things! Just ask the Garden Crew. They plant a garden and grow food that they get to eat. Taking care of a garden can be a lot of work, but it's also a lot of fun!